THE ONE AND ONLY
Super-Duper Golly-Whopper
JIM-DANDY REALLY-HANDY
CLOCK-TOCK-STOPPER

To Jesse, Melissa, William, Christopher, Lee,
Brian, Jared, Kyle, Matthew, and Amanda...
all my grandchildren so far.

P. T.

To Terase

J.O.

Text copyright © 1971 by Patricia Thomas
Illustrations copyright © 1990 by John O'Brien
All rights reserved. No part of this book may be reproduced or utilized
in any form or by any means, electronic or mechanical, including
photocopying, recording or by any information storage and retrieval
system, without permission in writing from the Publisher. Inquiries
should be addressed to Lothrop, Lee & Shepard Books, a division of
William Morrow & Company, Inc., 105 Madison Avenue, New York,
New York 10016. Printed in the United States of America.

First Edition   1 2 3 4 5 6 7 8 9 10

Library of Congress Cataloging in Publication Data
Thomas, Patty.
The one-and-only, super-duper, golly-whopper, jim-dandy, really-handy
clock-tock-stopper / by Patricia Thomas ; illustrated by John O'Brien.
p.   cm.   Summary: Seeking peace and quiet, Porcupine asks
Rabbit to stop his clock from ticking, with noisy results.
ISBN 0-688-09340-X.—ISBN 0-688-09341-8 (lib. bdg.)
[1. Clocks and watches—Fiction. 2. Noise—Fiction. 3. Porcupines—
Fiction. 4. Stories in rhyme.] I. O'Brien, John, 1953- ill.
II. Title. PZ8.3.T3160n 1990 [E]—dc20
89-13426 CIP AC

THE ONE AND ONLY
Super-Duper Golly-Whopper
JIM-DANDY REALLY-HANDY
CLOCK-TOCK-STOPPER

BY **PATRICIA THOMAS**

ILLUSTRATED BY **JOHN O'BRIEN**

Lothrop, Lee & Shepard Books   New York

Old gray, grouchy Porcupine
Lived in a house where the sun didn't shine,
A deep, dark hole
Once made by a mole,
Below the lumpy stump of a twisted pine.
And not a very happy soul
Was that porcupine.

No sir, he didn't like the stump; he didn't like the hole.
He hadn't even said "Thank you" to the mole.
(But then anyone who knew him would incline
To expect that of the porcupine.)
He was, you see, one who could never be quite content
No matter what he did or where he went.
In summer he got
Entirely too hot;
But in winter he'd be too cold, like as not.
Each day
He'd say
The sun was too bright.
But then, he'd contend it was too dark at night.
He was, in short,

The sort
Who would complain
Whether it did or did not rain.
He had no friends who'd stop by to play
Or ask, "How do you like the weather today?"
Why bother—they already knew what Porcupine would say!

So mostly he just stayed in his hole…by himself…
Alone except for his clock on the shelf.
He'd sit there in his rocker and rock
And grumble
And mumble
To his clock.
And the clock would answer simply, "Tick, tock."

Well, things went along pretty much this way,
Until one day
(When he could think of nothing else to complain about)
He vowed
His clock's tock was too loud
And let out
A shout!
"Clock," he cried, "I find it shocking
That you should prattle and rattle on with this constant tick-tocking!
Why, you make so much noise I can't hear myself think—
Let alone propose
To doze
Off a wink!"

"Tick, tock,"
Answered the clock.

So the porcupine shouted once more, in his loudest voice,
"Clock, I demand—
Yes, command—
You to stop this noise!"

The clock
Paid no attention. "Tick," it said firmly. "Tock."

The porcupine, not knowing what else to do,
Was in the process of removing his shoe,
Ready to throw it at the clock
When
Just then,
At his door he heard a knock.
As he opened it, in walked a rabbit, who tipped his hat
And said, "Sir, you don't know me, but I understand that
You have a problem—and I'm here to solve it.
Yes, dissolve it.

It seems this is your lucky day, for I just happen to have here in my
   bag the One and Only, Super-Duper, Golly-Whopper,
Jim-Dandy,
Really-Handy
Clock-Tock-Stopper.
Yes sir, and it comes with a written-down, money-back guarantee,
Plus a thirty-day trial which is absolutely free—
Except for a mere twenty-dollar deposit,
which you can leave right here with me."

Porcupine stared at him in shock
As the rabbit slipped an odd-looking object over the clock.
It was sort of a mass of gears and springs
And fluffy pillows tied on with strings,
Attached to the clock with a bar
Holding twenty-seven bees in a peanut-butter jar.

"I'll take that twenty dollars now," said the rabbit, skipping out the door.
Porcupine stood there, rooted to the floor.

The bees started to buzz and beat the air with their wings,
Which moved the gears; which sprung the springs;
Which tugged the pillows, tied with strings.
And now the clock said,
Buzzz…bizzz…
Whirrr…whizzz…
Boinggg…sproinggg…
Swoosh…whoosh…
TICK…tock…
TICK…tock.

"Hold on!" cried the porcupine. "There's something very much amiss
About all this.
Rabbit!" he called loudly. "How dare you disappear!
I insist you come back here
And fix this contraption you've put on my clock,
For now its tick is even louder than its tock!"

"Well, here I am," said the rabbit, bounding back into Porcupine's hole.
"I can see you have trouble. Yes, I can. Bless my soul!
And it's my fault, too. Yes it is, for I should have seen
That you couldn't stop your clock's tock with such a simple machine.
No sir, you need an attachment. You need the Snap-In, Quick-Fix,
   Custom-Sized Clock-Tock-Stopper-
Hopper-Popper—
And I just happen to have one. Mind you,
There's only one here that I could find you.
But it's all yours for only twenty dollars—including tax and handling fee,
Which I can hold for you, naturally."

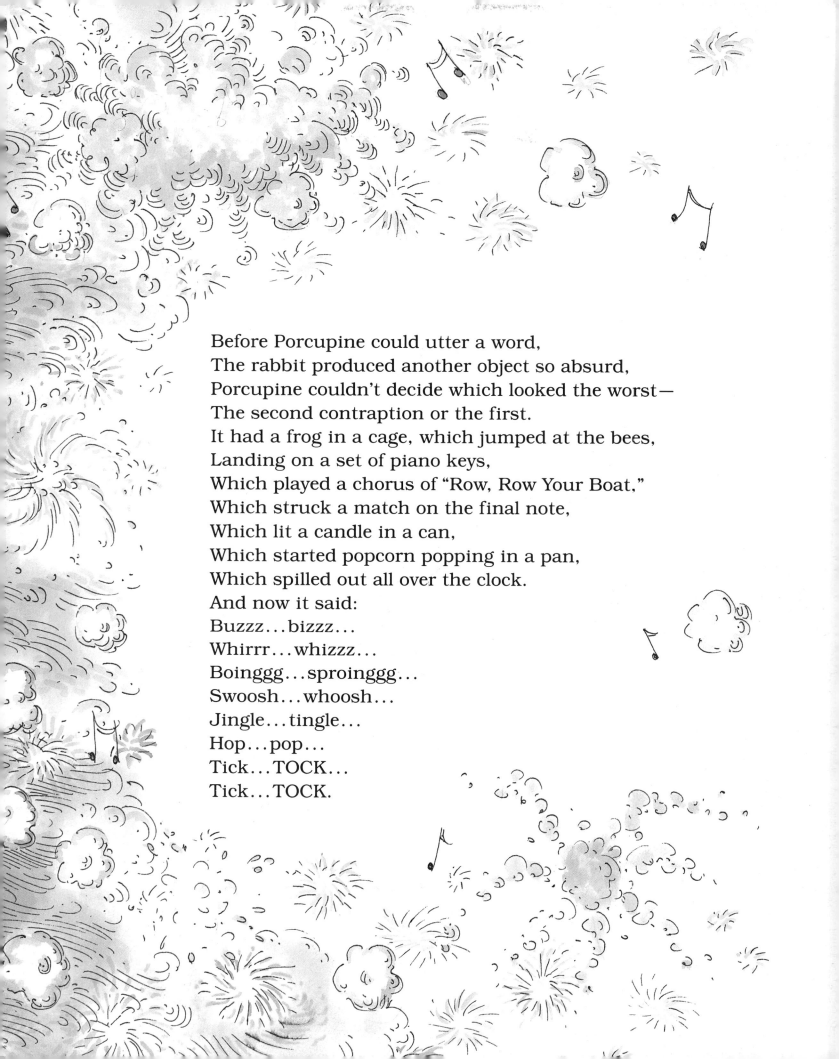

Before Porcupine could utter a word,
The rabbit produced another object so absurd,
Porcupine couldn't decide which looked the worst—
The second contraption or the first.
It had a frog in a cage, which jumped at the bees,
Landing on a set of piano keys,
Which played a chorus of "Row, Row Your Boat,"
Which struck a match on the final note,
Which lit a candle in a can,
Which started popcorn popping in a pan,
Which spilled out all over the clock.
And now it said:
Buzzz…bizzz…
Whirrr…whizzz…
Boinggg…sproinggg…
Swoosh…whoosh…
Jingle…tingle…
Hop…pop…
Tick…TOCK…
Tick…TOCK.

"Rabbit!" cried the porcupine.
"Come back this instant and fix this clock of mine!
Your gadgets aren't helping. In fact, they're harming,
And the situation is becoming alarming!"

"Alarming?" asked the rabbit. "Why, yes indeed.
An alarm is exactly what you need—
An alarm that will warn you when your clock
Is about to tick, or about to tock.
Well, don't you know I just happened to bring
Along with me the very thing.
And, of course, I absolutely guarantee
You'll be
Delighted with this great little accessory—
The best part of which is naturally that
You can wear it as a hat!
It's the First-Rate,
Just-Great
Clock-Tock-Stopper-
Hopper-Popper-
Fuzzer-Buzzer-Topper!
And it's on sale today only for the special low price
Of just twenty dollars. Isn't that nice!"

Before the porcupine could find his voice to speak,
The rabbit took his twenty dollars, tweaked his cheek,
And placed upon his head
An object of which it might well be said
That, although his head was the spot upon which it sat,
It looked very little like a hat.
It stuck out, right and left, in all directions,
With flashlight batteries and bulbs and wire connections,
And a scoop that caught the popping corn,
Tripping a switch that raised a horn,
Which blew several notes—long, loud, and clear—
And slipped a furry earmuff down over each ear.

The rabbit, brushing off his paws, turned to go.
Then suddenly he stopped and said, "Oh,
By the way, there's one more thing you should know.
This hat is also a radio!
It's a neat little feature you'll agree is clever,
Especially since it's yours at no extra cost whatsoever—
Except for a mere twenty dollars in rent,
Which you're sure to consider money well spent.
I'll take that now. No need to send a bill.
It will work just fine—as long as you sit very still."
With one quick
Flick
The rabbit turned the radio on—
And before Porcupine could speak, the rabbit was gone.

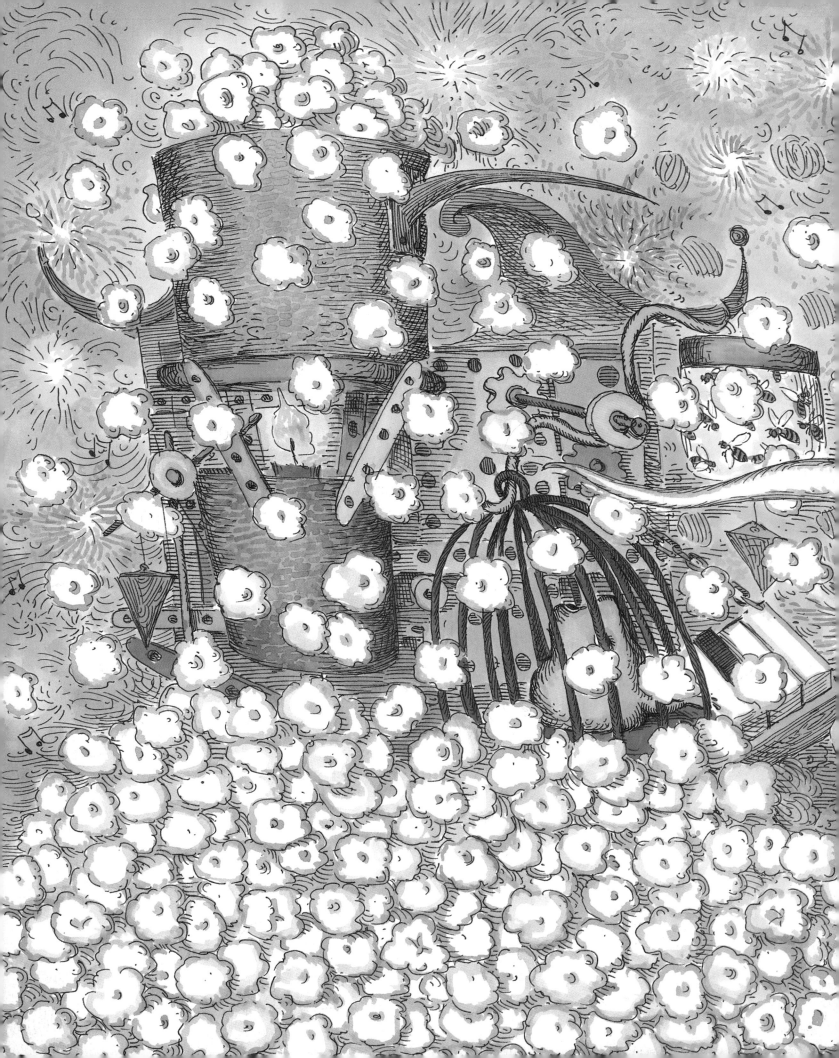

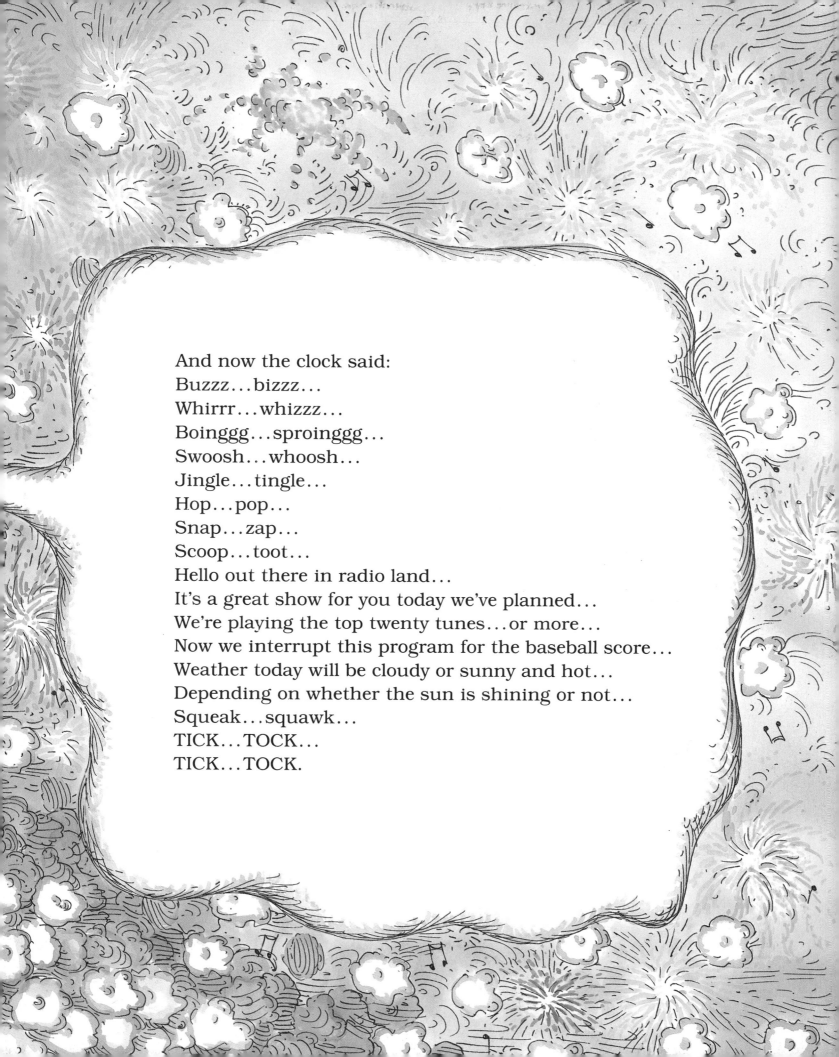

And now the clock said:
Buzzz…bizzz…
Whirrr…whizzz…
Boinggg…sproinggg…
Swoosh…whoosh…
Jingle…tingle…
Hop…pop…
Snap…zap…
Scoop…toot…
Hello out there in radio land…
It's a great show for you today we've planned…
We're playing the top twenty tunes…or more…
Now we interrupt this program for the baseball score…
Weather today will be cloudy or sunny and hot…
Depending on whether the sun is shining or not…
Squeak…squawk…
TICK…TOCK…
TICK…TOCK.

Porcupine put his paws to his ears and tore his hair
(Well, actually, he tore his quills, if you want to be perfectly
   accurate and fair),
And he tried
To hide
His head underneath his rocking chair.
But no matter which way he turned, the radio-hat
Prevented him from doing that.

Popcorn,
Popping
Without stopping,
Tumbled all over the floor,
While feathers from the pillows
In billows
Flew through the door.
The frog went bounding from table to shelf to chair.
Lights flashed,
The jar crashed,
And bees went buzzing off through the air,
Everywhere!

"Rabbit, Rabbit!" the porcupine screamed.
"I never, ever in my whole life dreamed
There could be such a smash-
Bash-
Mad-dashing
Hullaballooing!
I demand you come back and undo all you've been doing!"

"Why, my stars!" said the rabbit. "Am I to understand
That you consider the One and Only, Super-Duper, Golly-Whopper,
Jim-Dandy,
Really-Handy
Clock-Tock-Stopper something less than grand?
Now, don't you worry or fume or fret.
I'll take care of everything—on that you can bet.
Yes sir, for didn't I guarantee your satisfaction?
You can relax. I'm here to take action!"

With that, the rabbit whipped out a fan,
Which with one great thrust
Of a gust
Blew bees, frog, popcorn, and all into a can.
He snapped on the lid, clamped it down tight,
Stuffed it into his bag, and said, "All right,
Now I do
Recognize that a refund is due,
Which I'll be glad to put in the mail for you.

Or I can credit the whole amount
To your rather lengthy outstanding account,
Which should just about cover the standard clean-up and recovery fee—
And that leaves only twenty dollars that you still owe me.
I'll take it all in cash, now that I'm through.
It's been a real pleasure doing business with you!"

The rabbit tipped his hat, flicked his tie,
Picked up his bag, and was gone with a wave good-bye.

The porcupine could only look after him and stare.
Very slowly, he sank down into his rocking chair.
On the shelf, the little clock
Whispered softly, "Tick, tock."

"Well," sighed the porcupine, "upon my word,
I do believe the loveliest voice I've ever heard
Belongs to you, my dear little clock.
What a gentle tick! What a charming tock!
How quiet and cozy is my home here in this hole.
I must remember to drop a thank-you note to the mole.
Or perhaps I should visit him to ask if he's not altogether
Delighted with this cool-rainy, bright-sunny weather.
Though, on second thought, I'll ask first, so there'll be no doubt
That he has no Clock-Tock-Stopper about...."